A New Kind of Christmas

T. Lawren

SC Luxury Publishing

To those who continue to pursue their dream, no matter the obstacle.

You matter, your work matters, and your dreams matter.

INSPIRATIONAL WORKBOOKS

Refining Your Life Through the Fire

The Path to Purpose Following the Principles of God: Reflection Guide

INSPIRATIONAL

Dear Woman of God

The Path to Purpose Following the Principles of God

PLANNERS

Graced. Restored. Transformed.

FICTION

A New Kind of Thanksgiving

The story, all names, characters, and incidents portrayed in this production are fictitious. No identification with actual persons (living or deceased), places, buildings, and products is intended or should be inferred.

ISBN: (Paperback) 979-8-9928077-6-9

ISBN: E-Book) 979-8-9928077-5-2

Library of Congress Control Number: 2026903925

Author name: T. Lawren, 1984

Published by: SC Luxury Publishing

Imprint: SC Luxury Publishing

Website: www.tlawren.com

Contents

Chapter One

Aurora Denver kept her pace steady as she crossed the street, her breath rising in the cold morning air. Boston was already moving, already loud, already in full swing; and usually, she loved that. The noise, the energy, the rush... it felt familiar. It felt like home.

Today, it just felt like something she needed to get through.

She stepped into her office building, shaking off the snow, and glanced down at her phone. The reminder she'd tried to ignore flashed again.

Estate meeting — 10:30 AM.

Her stomach pulled tight.

Aunt Celeste.

She hadn't said the name out loud since the funeral, and she definitely wasn't ready for the meeting that came with it. But she went, because avoiding it wouldn't change anything.

The attorney was kind. Gentle. He walked her through everything slowly. Aurora nodded even though her mind drifted every few seconds. Hearing Celeste reduced to forms and signatures felt wrong.

Then came the condition.

When Aurora stepped back onto the sidewalk, the cold hit her harder than before.

Stay in Eden's Harbour through the holidays. Live in the cottage. And if she wanted to inherit it fully...She had to be married by Valentine's Day.

She stood still for several seconds, letting the traffic and voices blur around her.

Married? By Valentine's Day?! Her thoughts echoed

"Auntie... really?" she whispered.

It sounded like a joke, one Celeste wasn't here to tell her she was just kidding. Aurora wasn't even dating. She barely had time to water the plant in her apartment, let alone consider marriage.

She shoved her hands deeper into her coat pockets and started walking without any real direction. Her brain felt scrambled, trying to fit this strange condition into the life she'd built.

The cottage had meant everything to her when she was younger. It was the one place that felt peaceful, where she followed Celeste around the garden and listened to stories about love and independence and choosing your own life.

Aurora admired that about her aunt, maybe too much. She'd spent her twenties chasing that same independence, forgetting Celeste had also lived with regret she rarely talked about.

Now Aurora had to go back.

She paused at the corner and let out a long breath.

"Okay. I'll go," she said quietly. "I'll get through it."

A quick trip.

Handle the holidays.

Sign whatever needed to be signed. Figure out the rest later.

That was the plan.

But as she stood there, letting the cold settle around her, something tightened in her chest. She couldn't explain it. Grief, maybe. Annoyance. Confusion. All of it layered together in a way she didn't want to unpack.

Aurora shook her head, pushing the feeling away. She didn't have time to fall apart in the middle of the sidewalk.

She straightened her coat, adjusted her bag, and started walking toward the garage.

Boston would still be here when she got back. Nothing had to change.

At least, that's what she kept telling herself.

Unlocking her car, she climbed in. "Thank God for remote start, it is way too cold today." She said to herself while rubbing her hands together.

Aurora sat in silence, with only the faint sound of the engine running and the blow of the heater on high in her BMW M4.

She was replaying everything the lawyer said in her mind, stipulations and all. Still in a state of shock that her aunt would put *that* kind of clause in her will.

"What was she thinking? Did she really think I am that hard up and desperate for a man? UGH" she yelled out in frustration.

Her phone rings through the car speakers.

"Hey Maci", she said, sounding exhausted.

"Hi Aurora, sounds like you could use a break," Maci, her assistant said on the other end.

"You have no idea," she said, rolling her eyes.

"Well I'll be brief. I rescheduled your 2:00 appointment today, for tomorrow, your 4:00 I pushed back to 5:00, and Mark wants to know if you took a look at his proposal for the Walkins deal."

"Maci, you are the best I completely forgot about my afternoon schedule, I'm going to grab us lunch and be back at the office in a little."

"No worries. I know you had a lot to deal with today. I told you, to reschedule both for tomorrow."

"I know, next time I'll listen, you seem to know me better than I know myself anyway, " she chuckled lightly."

"It's my job to know you. I'm sure you'd fire me if I didn't."

Aurora laughs, "I would never. Oh and tell Mark if he wants in on the Walkins deal, I have some notes on his proposal"

"Will do. Anything else you need before you get back?"

Aurora paused.

She sighed. "Yes, can you call the charter company and see what flights are available for next week? I have to go home to Maine."

"Sure thing, what's the tentative return date?"

"I don't even know at this point."

"Huh?"

"Oh I'll explain when I get back."

"Okay, see you when you get here. be safe."

"Will do, bye."

As the call disconnects Aurora shifts into drive and makes her way through the traffic. Feeling her thoughts drift back to her aunt, she presses the voice button on her steering wheel. “Hey Sirus , play Highway Vibe playlist on Avocado music.”

When the Beat Drops for ‘Get It Shawty’ by Lloyd, Aurora turns up the volume, starts to sing along and forgets about what's waiting for her next week.

“That's tomorrow's issue, today I'm gone... get it shorty.” she laughs as she whips through traffic, heading to pick up her and Maci's food, then back to the office.

CHAPTER TWO

"Aurora," Maci calls out.

Silence

"Aurora," she calls again.

Silence

"Miss Denver!"

Aurora snaps her head up. "I'm sorry Maci, I checked out for a minute."

"I see," Maci chuckled. "Well, Mark dropped off his proposal again. he said he took your notes into consideration."

Aurora rolled her eyes. “That means he didn't make any changes, let me at least look at it again before I say no,” she laughs reaching for the portfolio Maci was holding.

“He really wants in on the Walkins deal huh?”

“No, he wants in on that $100,000 Christmas bonus the Walkins gives to the team that works their design project. I love that they do that for the team but it's exhausting when I have to filter through subpar proposals,” she says flipping the pages of Marks’ proposal.

“I can understand that.” Maci sympathizes.

“And the Walkins have been doing this every year since I took them on as clients, they're just so...”

“Eccentric.” Maci chuckled.

Aurora laughs. “ yeah we'll go with that. because who redecorates their entire house every year.”

“Probably me, if I had the money.” Maci laughed.

“Maci, I have the money and still won't do it.”

Maci placed her hand on Aurora’s shoulder. “I've seen your apartment. You have no room to talk.”

“Yes, but I keep with the same theme.”

“Mhm. Since you are leaving this weekend, are you going to choose the the team before you go?”

“Ugh. You just *had* to ruin the moment.” Aurora leaned back in her chair.

Maci laughed. “I know but with you going to Maine, and not having a tentative return date, it's best to choose now. Please don't leave me here without choosing, or take me with you.”

“I wouldn't do that to you Maci. And if I didn't think your husband would kill me, I'd definitely take you with me. I might need the backup.”

“Say the word and I'm packing a bag, him and those munchkins of mine would be just fine.”

“Ummm, no ma'am. But thanks for the offer. I'm going to give the Walkins deal to Melanie, Joel, Mark, and you.”

Maci's eyes widened, “What do you mean me?”

“Maci please, you are an excellent designer. You've been with me since the start of this company, you know the Walkins’ inside and out. You've got this, and you're running point on the deal, so I know it will be perfect."

"Yes ma'am. But you're actually going to let Mark on the deal this year? You never choose him."

Aurora hands her the portfolio. "Take a look and tell me what you see."

Maci flips through the pages, "Hmm. Wow, well okay. He actually took your notes and changed his proposal."

"And that's why I chose him. He's finally learning to be a team player. Plus he really does have a great eye for design, he wouldn't be at this firm if he didn't. All of you are the reason I have one of the top design firms in Boston."

"Yes indeed. Since you won't be here during the meeting while you're back home, do you want me to conference you in?"

"There you go ruining the mood again," Aurora laughs. "But no, you don't have to. I trust your judgment. you can call me and let me know what crazy thing they come up with this year."

"Will do."

"And lean into Melanie and Joel if Mark tries to give you any push-back. he's the rookie on the team, not you and Mellie and Joel will definitely remind him and have your back."

"Okay. Oh and I checked, the pilot filed the plan; flight takes off at 10:00AM."

"And let me guess, there still no direct route to Eden's harbor?"

"Nope. You will have a car waiting in Portland to take you the rest of the way."

"I'm hating this more by the minute. Will I at least have my favorite pilot?"

"Yes, Captain Reynolds is flying you."

Aurora sighed. "Well there's some good news in there, finally."

"Exactly, so stop complaining. This may just be what you need anyway. You constantly go non-stop, maybe your aunt was on to something by having you go down there."

"Maci, I don't think forcing me to get married in order to retain her home is a good thing though."

Maci laughs, "Honestly Aurora, I think it may be more to it than that. This just seems so random."

"Trust me it's not. You had to have known my aunt. She is serious."

"Well, I'm sure you are going to be fine Aurora. You really need the time away. I know you are finalizing family business, but please prioritize yourself while you're there."

"I'll make you a deal, I'll go to Maine with an open mind, if you show everyone what skills you've been hiding as my assistant, and why I really chose you to run point on this deal."

"I can do that."

"Great. Now can you get everyone in the conference room. I'll be there in about 30 minutes. That should give you all time to finish putting together that impromptu Christmas party."

Maci's eyes widened. "You're not going to be here for the annual party and I just –"

"I know Maci", she smiled, "Thank you. I love it and I can make the team choice announcement there too."

"Awesome," she lightly jumped as she hurried out of the office closing the door behind her.

Aurora pulled out her phone and scroll to her aunts' contact. Affectionately named, Auntie Mom.

Staring at her picture. "I really can't believe you are doing this to me. It's bad enough you left, now you're making me get married, and by Valentine's day? When did you even become this person auntie? Ugh. I guess this is my punishment for not coming home the last few years. Is that what this is?"

She sighs. "Ugh. If it was anyone else, I'd say forget it. Only for you."

She smiled, looking out her window.

"You always knew how to make an entrance and for sure and exit. When I make it to heaven, you and I are going to have a talk." she laughed.

Locking her phone, Aurora stood up, buttoned her blazer and headed to the conference room.

Chapter Three

The wind met Aurora the moment the car door open, cold and sharp against her cheeks, and she stepped on to the tarmac. The sleek white jet bearing the gold and char-coaled emblem of Meridian Elite Aviation waited ahead of her, it stairs already lowered.

A flight attendant stood at the top of the stairs with a warm smile. "Welcome aboard Miss Denver, I'm Elaine. I can take your bag for you," she greeted as Aurora began ascending the stairs.

"Good morning, yes thank you," she said handing her the bag she was carrying.

As Aurora continues to ascend the stairs, she paused and looked out at the city she was leaving behind, let out a long sigh and continued walking up the stairs.

Taking her seat, the flight attendant approached her, “Miss Denver, would you prefer a coffee or mimosa?”

Aurora rubbed her head, “For this trip, I'll take the mimosa please, then I'll take the coffee.”

Elaine chuckled, “Yes ma'am, I'll have that right out to you.”

Aurora pulled out her laptop to take a look at some of the designs that had been submitted by her team.

“Well if it isn't my favorite passenger,” Captain Reynolds smiles as he walks out of the cockpit.

Aurora takes a sip of her mimosa. “Oscar, you know I am not your favorite passenger, but you *are* my favorite pilot.”

Oscar laughs, and holds his hand over his heart. “So much love for little old me.”

“You are too much. How's your family?”

“They are great, we just had another baby, and see this is why you are my favorite, you're the only one who asks about my family."

“Another? You're aiming to have an entire team I see.”

“Hey, somebody's got to take care of me when I get too old to fly. So Maine, huh? Finally taking a break?”

Aurora shifted in her seat. “Forced one. My aunt passed and she had this crazy stipulation in her will. Now I have to go to that small town and wrap some things up.” She motions to Elaine for another mimosa.

Oscar chuckles. “You might want to take it easy, it's a short flight.”

Aurora nods her head and takes a sip. “Which is why I'm having coffee after this,” she tilts her glass to him.

“Oh boy,” Oscar laughs as he heads back to the cockpit, “look at it this way, whatever it is you have to do, may just be exactly what you need.”

“I doubt it,” she mumbled to herself, "thanks Oscar.”

“No problem. And you know my rule, short flights means no working. Laptop away and relax please.”

“Oscar...”

“The same work will be there when you land, TAKE A BREAK, Miss Denver."

Conceding, Aurora put her laptop away. “Fine Oscar, fine!”

“Thank you kindly, and enjoy the flight.” He says with a wink and a smile as he closes the cockpit door.

Aurora leans back in her chair. "Elaine, once we're in the air, can I get that cup of coffee please?”

“Sure thing Miss Denver,” as she takes her seat and straps in.

Aurora looked out the window and watched the runway disappear as the plane ascended. She focused in on the city, her home, disappearing.

She was leaving behind the busyness of Boston, where she thrived. As the lights of the city became but a mere twinkle, she felt a tightening in her chest.

Aurora couldn't help but wonder if taking claim of what she knew as her family home, was worth the trouble.

As the plane leveled off she unbuckled her seat and stretched as Elaine approached her with a coffee mug. “ Here you go Miss Denver.”

“Thank you Elaine,” she takes a sip, “Oh this is perfect.”

Elaine smile satisfied, “I do my best.”

Aurora reaches for her laptop.

“I'm sorry Miss Denver. Captain Reynolds said to remind you of his, 'no work' rule, if you pulled out your laptop.”

Aurora softly laughs.” really Oscar?”

“It's not that long of a flight. How about I dim the lights and you can get a nap in instead?”

“I guess that's the only thing I *can* do.”

“Great, and this was dropped off before you arrived.” Elaine hands her a gift bag.

A note card sat on top of the tissue paper.

"Oh Maci," she takes out the tissue paper to reveal an eye mask and matching blanket.

"It looks like someone else wants you to sleep, ma'am." Elaine said as she dim the lights.

Stretching out into her seat and covering herself with a blanket, Aurora laughs. "Well, I guess I will listen, wake me when we get ready to land please," as she slides the eye mask over her eyes and nestles herself to sleep.

Elaine gently Taps Aurora's shoulder." Miss Denvers, we've landed."

Aurora sat up straight, removing her eye mask. "I wanted to be woken up before we landed."

Elaine eyeing her with worry. " yes, I know, but–"

"But I told her to let you sleep." Oscar interrupted. "This is the longest you have slept on any of my flights and this was your shortest flight. You needed the rest Aurora."

Aurora visibly upset, "that may be Oscar, but I wanted to freshen up and have a coffee before I got off the plane."

"And you can still do that, we made great time. We're almost an hour ahead of schedule, and your car isn't here yet. So calm down, freshen up, have your coffee and relax, you have time."

Her countenance relaxing, Aurora replied. "You really are my favorite pilot you know that?"

"I know, I'm the only one that can deal with you." he laughed.

"Oh hush, she laughed and she walked to the restroom.

"Okay Aurora, you going to get to Eden's Harbor, figure out a way around this stipulation and get back to your life in Boston. You will not get stuck in this town."

Aurora finished her pep talk and freshening up, went back to her seat, and grabbed her laptop.

"No time for work, your car is here." Oscar laughed.

Aurora looked up. "I haven't even had my coffee yet."

“I have it right here Mis Denver. All ready for your car ride.”

“Well, it seems like you two are trying to get rid of me, so I'll be on my way,” she laughed.

“Not at all Miss Denver, but do enjoy your stay.” Elaine smile as she handed Aurora her bag.

“I will see you on the return flight, Oscar." Aurora called out as she descended the stairs.

“We'll see, Aurora, we'll see. Enjoy the ride home, and remember to expect the unexpected.”

Aurora paused at the bottom of the stairs, taking in what Oscar said and sighed.

She surveyed her surroundings as she walked toward the car that was waiting on the tarmac. Her preferred car service was waiting, thankfully Portland had it, the driver was standing near the rear door and opened it as she approached.

“Welcome to Portland, Miss Denver, I'm Kenny.”

“Hi Kenny, thank you,' she said as she slid into the backseat of the black sedan, the door closing softly.

She smiled, noticing her usual brand of water in the center console. It was the attention to detail that kept her using the same company. Kenny slid in the driver seat," It's a bit of a drive to Eden's Harbor ma'am. There's a charger for your phone and outlet for your laptop under the console."

"Thank you Kenny."

"Something wrong?" noticing the change in her tone.

"Other than I'd rather stay here in Portland than go to the slowest and smallest city in Maine."

Kenny laughed," Well Miss Denver, I'm not sure the last time you've been to Eden's Harbor, but it has definitely changed it is not as small as you may think."

"Any changes they have made, I'm sure it still doesn't compare to Portland, let alone Boston." she said rolling her eyes.

Kenny chuckled as he shifted to drive," I guess you will have to see for yourself." He drove off the tarmac and began the two hour drive to Eden's Harbor.

Aurora pulled out her phone to text Maci.

Landed, on the way to BORING CITY!

Stop it. Glad you made it safely.

Is Mark giving you any pushback yet?

Nothing I can't handle.

Thank you for my gift.

You're welcome. But did you use it on the plane?

Yes, I was forced to.

Good. LOL, once you get to the house I'll give you a call with an update on this project.

Sounds good. Talk soon.

She checked a few emails, then put her phone away. Remembering what Kenny said about changes, she decided to keep an eye on the scenery, to see her for herself what actually changed. As he merged on the highway, she saw the sign that read Eden's Harbor 123 miles, thinking, this will give her time to try and come up with some alternatives to her aunts' will, or at the very least figure out a way out of the marriage part.

Aurora grab the water and took a sip—ice cold— just like she liked it, and took in the scenery. It was lightly snowing, the landscaping on the side of the highway turning white.

She relaxed more in her seat and began to plot her escape of the town, before she even arrived.

Chapter Four

Aurora felt the car come to a stop after a few hours. She looked out of the car window and sighed. The house looks bigger than she remembered. " I don't know why Auntie called this a cottage, it's way too big." she said out loud.

"You're right about that Miss Denver," Kenny chuckled," this is too big to be called a cottage." He opened the door and headed to the trunk to unload her bags.

Aurora watched Kenny as he brought her luggage up to the front door and walk back to the car. She felt a lump in her throat and her heart sink deeper into her chest as he opened her door, extending his hand to help her out of the car.

“Thank you Kenny. I appreciate the great time. And thank you for being bringing my bags to the door.”

“No thanks necessary ma'am.” Kenny smiled and tipped his hat as he walked back to the car. “Enjoy your time home, and if you need a car service just call the regular number and ask for Kenny. I live just outside the harbor.”

Aurora smiled. "Will do, Kenny. Thank you again.” she waved as he drove off. She watched the car disappeared down the street, then turned to walk to the house.

“Rora Jean, is that you?”

Aurora turned around in shock. She hadn't been called that name in years.

“Mrs. Cole made her way up the snow covered sidewalk. That *is* you Rora Jean, come here and give me a hug girl,” she didn't wait for an answer, as she pulled Aurora into a hug.

Aurora gasped from Mrs. Cole's tight embrace, she took a step back when she released her. “Hi Mrs. Cole.” she said with a forced smile.

“Oh, I'm Mrs. Cole, now? You done went off to the big city and forgot that since you could talk, I was Auntie Bren. Well, I guess years of you not coming home will do that." she faked a disappointed look.

Aurora smiled, "I'm sorry Auntie Bren," she hugged her again. "I was just caught off guard, I haven't been called Rora Jean in forever."

"Mhm, it's alright baby. Had you not shot out of here so fast after Celeste's funeral, you would have heard that name quite a bit."

"Auntie Bren," Aurora sighed loudly.

Mrs. Cole raised up her hands in surrender. "Okay baby, I'm sorry."

"You could at least let me get in the house and settled before you start fussing." Aurora laughed as she unlocked the door.

"And since when have you known for me to give anyone a chance, before I fuss at them?" Mrs. Cole said as she grabbed one of Auroras bags to carry in.

Aurora, seeing her grabbing a bag, reached out for it, "Auntie Bre, I can–"

“Move girl,” she waved her off, “I may be older than you, but I’m far from helpless. Now come on in this house before you catch cold!”

Aurora closed the door behind them and rolled her eyes. “You know Auntie Bren, It’s been a long day already, I really just want to take a minute to rest.”

“Okay baby. I can take a hint. I’ll leave you be and let you get settled.”

“Thanks Auntie.” Aurora smiled.

Mrs. Cole grabbed her hand and pulled her into a hug. “I’m really glad to see you baby. Don’t you keep yourself cooped up in this house the whole time you’re here. Go out in the town, a lot has changed since you lived here.”

“I saw that on my way in. And I won’t stay in the house. I have some things to take care of while I’m here.”

“Okay good. Well, I’ll be seeing you.”

Aurora waved to Mrs. Cole as she made her way down the sidewalk and back home. She went back inside, stood with her back against the front door and let out a heavy sigh.

"Well," she said running her fingers through her curls, "I'll guess I'll unpack." Walking down the hall to her old room, her eyes began to linger on the pictures lined up on either side of the hallway. Family photos of her and Auntie Mom through the years. The hallway seemed to go on forever until she reached her room.

As she opened the door and stepped in, she realized her aunt had made a few updates, but kept her room relatively the same. Her barbie collectibles were still there, but now were on a custom built shelf, displaying each one.

All of her stuffed animals were nestled neatly on her bay window sitting area. Best of all, her princess canopy bed was still set up and still looked brand new. Auntie Mom had updated her room, but still kept her childhood nostalgia in tact.

Aurora sat her suitcase on the sofa that had been added in front of her bed. She paused and took in everything, the look, the smell, the memories. She took a picture off of the dresser and smiled as tears began to well up in her eyes.

Holding the picture of her parents, her at five years old, and Celeste, she took in their big smiles they had, and the realization that she is the only one left. Her parents were killed in a car accident three months after that picture was taken and she came to live with Celeste.

Although her parents were gone, Celeste never let their memory fade. Aurora grew up knowing everything about them. Looking at the picture now, she sees that she was the splitting image of her mom.

A tear dropped.

Aurora sat the picture face down on the dresser and wiped her eyes. "Nope. I am not doing this." She stormed out of the room. "This is exactly why I didn't want to come here. UGH!

"And when did this house get so big?!" she yelled out in frustration.

"I should have stayed in a hotel. On top of being in this Godforsaken town, and this house, *now* I have to deal with Auntie Bren's pushy self, and Auntie Mom expects me, *ME*, to get married to keep this house? For what? I don't even want to live here. And I definitely don't want to spend the holidays here. Why did I even agree to come?"

"Great, now I'm talking to myself and expecting an answer. I need to get out of here. I need my laptop and a drink, and I know Mrs.

'I love the Lord' doesn't have anything in here. And I bet there's nothing good in this town. Ugh." She ran her palm across her face.

"Calm down Aurora," she said to herself as she pinched the side of her pants, her method of self soothing.

"Take a breath and think, what do you actually need?" Aurora let out a deep sigh and began to calm herself.

She heard a light tap at the door. Aurora opened it and Mrs. Cole stood there with her hands up, "I come in peace baby."

Aurora stepped to the side and let her in.

"That's okay baby. I'm just here to feed you." she handed her a bag. "There's a salmon dinner in there from one of the best seafood restaurants here, and a dessert sample tray from my favorite bakery in town, and this bottle of wine.

Her eyes lit up, "Thank you Auntie Bren. I really appreciate this."

"No problem baby, now you eat up and get you some rest. Tomorrow is a new day. Ima get going, I got pies in the oven. I'll see you later baby."

Aurora smiled as she went to the kitchen to get a plate. "Oh I hope this tastes as good as it looks and smells."

After she poured her glass of wine, she sat down to eat. "Oh my God," she took another bite. "Okay, whoever the chef is there, definitely did their thing."

Taking a sip of wine, she paused. "What is this?" she grabbed the bottle and read, "Non alcoholic, seriously Aunt Bren." she laughed. "Well at least it's not nasty."

Finishing her meal, she cleaned her dishes and opened the box of desserts. "These look amazing. I think I'll try this one. Mmmm now that's a lemon tart. She looked at the logo o the box, "Tianna's Bistro & Cafe. Yeah, I will be paying them a visit. I guess I can take a look around this town while I'm here. But first," she grabbed her phone to check in with Maci.

No answer.

Hey Maci, how are things going? Apparently you're ignoring my calls.

Lol. I'm not. I'm with the Walkins right now. CRAZY, is all I can say about them.

Yep, that sounds about right. You've got this.

Thanks, we'll be with them a while, I'll call you to tell you about it.

Okay, looking forward to it.

Putting her phone on the charger, Aurora took a shower, brushed her teeth and climbed into bed. "Tomorrow is a new day and I am finding a way out of this will." She turned off her bedside lamp, pulled her eye-mask down and drifted into sleep.

CHAPTER FIVE

The sun rays beamed in illuminating the entire room as Aurora sat up and stretched. She looked over at her phone.

10:15am

“Crap! I was supposed to be up at 6. I have too much to do to be sleeping in.”

Jumping out of the bed, she grabbed her phone, dials out and the car service picks up after one ring. “Good morning, this is Aurora Denver, is Kenny available today?”

“Yes ma’am, he is.”

“Great. I’d like to reserve a car for the day as soon as possible.”

“Yes ma’am. He'll be there at 11:15.”

“Thank you.”

She couldn’t put her finger on it, but something was different today. She had never slept in before, even after a long flight and jet lag, she was always up at the crack of dawn, coffee in hand, ready to take on the business of Boston. Today seemed like it was a bit slower, like she didn’t have to rush.

Shrugging of whatever it was, she finished getting ready and waited for Kenny to arrive.

The doorbell rang, she grabbed her purse and headed to the door.

“Good morning ma’am.” Kenny tipped his hat.

“Good morning Kenny,” she said with a smile following him to the car, and sliding into the backseat as he held the door open.

Kenny hopped into the front seat. “Where to today?”

“First, I need coffee and breakfast. There’s a law firm I need to go to, some apparel shops, because apparently it’s way colder than what I was expecting. I also want to see about getting a rental while I’m here. Hopefully, we don’t have to go all the way to Portland to get a nice car.”

"No," Kenny chuckled, "there's a local place that has the high end cars I'm sure you are used to. And I know the perfect place for coffee and breakfast." he smiles as he turns out of the driveway.

As they drove through downtown, Aurora admired the Christmas decorations and banners hanging. "Wow, this town sure does go all out for Christmas."

Kenny laughed, "Not just Christmas, all of the holidays. Just wait until you see everything lit up at night. It's beautiful ma'am."

"I bet it is," she smiled, remembering how her Aunt Celeste would drive her through different neighborhoods to look at Christmas lights.

"After you get your car, you should take a drive and really see all of the decorations."

"I just might, depending on how the day goes."

"Yes ma'am. Well here we are, best place in town for breakfast, coffee, and something sweet."

She peered out of the window and looked at the sign, *Tianna's Bistro & Cafe*. "Oh this is the place my aunt brought me desserts from, they sell breakfast too?"

"Yes ma'am," he opened her door. "The best you'll have."

Aurora stepped out and looked down the sidewalk at all of the businesses, and people. She even spotted a bookstore across the street. "Wow, it...it looks really great out here. It's definitely bigger and more alive than I remember."

She stepped inside of the bistro and her stomach growled as soon as the scents of fresh baked goods invaded her nostrils.

Waiting in line, she eyed the menu and listened to the softness of the voice of the woman taking orders. She sounded like she loved what she was doing, which reminded her of Aunt Celeste.

As she read the menu she saw a note, *Encouragement of the day: 'Be anxious for nothing, but instead, seek guidance and peace.'*

"Wow."

"Figured out what you want yet?" Kenny asked behind her.

"You know, I can't decide. What would you recommend?"

"It depends on what you're in the mood for, and don't take any food recommendations from him, he'll have you buying everything." a young girl came up beside them.

Kenny gasped. "I would *absolutely* do that."

“Exactly, Uncle Kenny!” Tianna laughed, rolling her eyes and hugging him.

“I’m Tianna,” she said, extending her hand to Aurora, “you must be visiting here, dressed like that.” she smiled.

Rebekah swatted at her arm. “Tianna hush, don’t mind her, what she meant was, welcome to our shop. What can we get you?”

Aurora looked down at her clothes. “Is it that obvious?’

“You do look like you just stepped out of a luxury magazine, but nothing is wrong with that. One of my best friends dresses like that all of the time. So what are you in the mood for?" Rebekah smiled.

“Well in Boston, I’d always get a caramel macchiato with triple espresso and a turkey, cheese, and spinach croissant, but I don't see that on your menu.”

Rebekah paused. “I’ve got the perfect thing for you. Have a seat and I‘ll bring it out soon.”

Kenny raised his arms. “What about me?”

"Your food is in the warmer, big brother. Tiana, go get your uncle’s food.”

"Big brother huh? Now Kenny, are you recommending this place because its family?" Aurora smiled.

Kenny laughed. "No ma'am. I take my job and recommendations seriously, the best place just happens to be my sisters'. You'll see."

Aurora noticed a sign on the bulletin board. "Christmas Jubilee, what's that?"

"That," Rebekah says as she sits Aurora's food in front of her, "is a fancy way of saying Christmas party. It's a week before Christmas, if you're still here you should come. Now tell me, what do you think of your coffee and food?"

Aurora takes a bite of the oversized croissant. She didn't say a word, just grabbed her coffee and took a sip. She smiled. "I think Ihave found my new breakfast spot.

Rebekah smiled. "That's good to hear. I'll leave you to it."

"Okay Miss Denver, I'll leave you to your breakfast. I'll be at the car when you're ready."

"Thank you Kenny, I won't be long. Busy day ahead."

Kenny tipped his hat as he walked out.

Aurora went back to her croissant and coffee. “This really is delicious, and just what I needed.”

She felt her phone buzzing in her Birkin Bag. Pulling it out, “Finally,” she said before answering.

“Hi Maci, I thought I was going to have to fly back, to hear from you.”

Maci chuckled. “Now Aurora, please stop the madness.”

"Well, I’ve been waiting on an update from your meeting with the Walkins.”

"I’m afraid you’ll still have to wait on that. I found the law firm you need to go to, it’s Parker & Steele Law. You have a 10:30 appointment with Katelyn Parker.”

Aurora checked her watch. “Maci that’s in forty five minutes!"

"I know, I’m sorry. The office said that’s the only availability until after the new year.”

"That’s fine. I’m already out, I was just hoping for a later time. Thanks Maci, I’ll talk to you later.”

Aurora hurriedly finished her food and headed out of the door, thanking Rebekah for the service.

Kenny had the car door open waiting for her. "I just learned I have a 10:30 appointment at Parker & Steele Law, is that far from here?"

"No ma'am, about a 15 minute drive into the busier part of town."

"Okay great."

"Miss Parker will see you now."

Aurora followed the secretary into a large open office, where a young and stern looking woman was sitting behind her desk. She stood and greeted her with a firm handshake.

"Hello Miss Denver, have a seat."

"Thank you for seeing me on such short notice."

"Of course. I am sorry about your loss. I did review your aunts' will as asked." She stated getting straight to business. "Unfortunately there are no loopholes, what she has stated here is binding. The only way for you to take claim of the home is following her instructions. There is, however, a clause that wasn't in your copy of the will, it was filed locally."

Aurora perked up. "A clause?"

"Yes, if you decide not to follow through, the home will become property of the state, and you can choose to buy it back, at cost, then."

"So instead of inheriting it, I would have to buy it? How long does that take?"

"Your aunt was very meticulous in this, it would remain as part of her estate for one year, after that, it can be put on the market. But, let me be frank, homes in that area, rarely go up for sale. If they do, they are sold the same day it is listed. There's no guarantee you would even get it."

Aurora leaned back and sighed, feeling defeated. "I just..." her thought trailed off.

"Look, take it from someone who was born and raised here. It's not that bad of a place. Trust me, there is more here than downtown and where your aunt lived. If there wasn't, I would not be here at all."

Aurora feigned a smile. "Thank you for your time, Miss Parker." She stood, shook her hand, and walked out of the office feeling as if the walls were closing in on her.

She made her way to the car waiting for her. "Ready to go pick out a car Miss Denver?" Kenny asked with his usual charm.

"No Kenny, I think I'd rather go back to the house," she said solemnly.

"Yes ma'am," as he drove off.

Chapter Six

A week had passed and Aurora had not stepped foot out of house.

She'd turn her phone off and would only respond to her team by email. Had it not been for Mrs. Cole leaving care packages at the door, she wouldn't have eaten. She sat in the house in anger and frustration.

"Is this what you wanted Auntie Mom? You wanted me to go crazy? How is it that beyond the grave, you want to force me back here and then force me to get married? You weren't married and you were just fine! Ugh!"

She looked at her aunt's bedroom door, the one room she hadn't gone into since coming back to the house.

"Why would you do this to me? I don't want to stay here! But, I don't want to lose your house. This *was* my home once!"

She paced back and forth in front of her door. "What? You want me to pray now? You want me to talk to God? God only heard you, not me. If he heard me, you would still be here!"

Tears dropped from her eyes as she got closer to her aunts' room. She reached out for the doorknob, then pulled her hand back.

"This is stupid," she said wiping her tears, "it's just a room."

Reaching for the doorknob again, this time opening the door, she peered into the room. Everything the same as it was before Celeste died. There was a basket of clothes sitting on the edge of the bed. Her desk lamp was still on and her Bible open.

Aurora stepped into the room walking toward the walk-in closet, running her hands along he dresses that were hanging. She pulled out one of the blouses and breathed in the familiar scent of her aunt that lingered.

"I really miss you Auntie Mom, and *man* did you have style." she smiled through her tear filled eyes.

She sat down at her desk and looked at the framed photo of the two of them. "I guess I'll have to accept defeat, I don't want someone else to have our home." As she sighed and leaned back, she caught a glimpse of herself in the mirror. "Oh. Girl you look a mess! Do something with yourself." she laughed.

"Whew, there is nothing better than a long, hot aromatherapy shower!"

She checked herself out in the mirror. "Now that's how you are supposed to look, fierce. Now let's see what the day brings."

Sh grabbed her keys to the rental car Maci had delivered, a couple of days ago.

"Thank you Maci for knowing me so well." She said to no one.

She opened the door and almost jumped out of her skin. "Auntie Bren, you almost gave me a heart attack. What are you doing here?"

"I just came to check on you baby. I haven't seen or heard from you in over a week."

"I'm okay. I was just headed out though."

"Well that's perfect, care to take an old woman on a few errands?"

Aurora sighed. “Yes ma’am. I guess taking you around is a good way to relearn my way around.”

"Yes it is, and I get to ride around in that new car of yours.”

"Now is that the real reason you have me playing chauffeur,” she laughed as she locked the door.

Mrs. Cole smiled, “Why yes...yes it is. Now baby, you look really good, very stylish, but you are going to need a thicker coat.”

"I know, Auntie Bren, that’s one of the reasons I was getting out today. I’m going shopping.”

"Good. I don’t need you freezing to death on my watch,” she laughed as he climbed into the passenger seat of Aurora's polar white AMG G63. “This looks like a vehicle *you* would drive, stylish and over the top. Just like Celeste.”

"And I’ll be taking that as a compliment, she said as she started the car. “Now where to?”

Now Auntie Bren when you said a few errands, I didn't think you'd have me all over town, and out over three hours." Aurora fussed pulling into valet parking at a restaurant in The Heights.

"Oh hush girl. At least I'm treating you to lunch."

Aurora smiled, "Well there's that," as she reached for her valet ticket.

As they were seated, Aurora admired the restaurant decor and layout. "This kind of reminds me of one of the restaurants back in Boston.

"I told you there was more to this town than you remember."

"It's definitely bigger and has more upscale shops and restaurants than I would have thought."

"I knew taking you to Laura's boutique would be the best first stop. With how you dress, that was definitely the perfect place."

"You know, you have been taking shots at the way I dress all day. But I'm still taking it as a compliment," she laughed, looking over her menu.

"It *is* a compliment baby. You dress very well, just a little...."

"A little what?" Aurora eyed her.

"Well baby, you dress like you are going to a fancy dinner party everyday," she chuckled.

"So you're saying I overdress?"

"I'm saying you are stylish. Don't change how you dress on account of me."

"Oh, I wasn't. I was just wondering if that's how everyone here sees me."

Mrs. Cole gently grabbed her hand. "No baby, I'm just teasing you. Besides, Laura, the owner of the boutique, dresses the same way, you'll fit right in.

The waitress comes and takes their orders, then a silence falls between them.

Aurora looks off into the distance and her mind drifts back to why she's here.

"Aurora baby." Mrs. Cole starts.

Silence

"Aurora..." she tries again.

Nothing

"Now young lady, I know you are not ignoring me." She says a bit more stern.

She finally snaps out of it. "I'm sorry Auntie Bren. What happened?"

"Nothing happened, but what's got you so distracted?"

"I've just got a lot on my mind Auntie."

Mrs. Cole paused for a moment. "You know baby, I know you are used to being alone and dealing with thins yourself. But while you are here, let me help you, if not me, at least bring it to the Lord."

"Auntie, I —"

The waitress walks up with their food, and Aurora uses it as an opportunity to change the subject.

"Wow, this looks great," she digs into her food.

"Mhmm. It does." Mrs. Cole took note of the subject change, but decided not to press.

Their conversation through lunch continued with Mrs. Cole giving more run downs of the town, the updates, the people, a bit of everything. They finished their meals, paid and headed out the door.

"You know," Ms. Cole said with a smile, "the towns Christmas Jubilee is this weekend. You want to be your auntie's escort?"

"Auntie Bren, I hadn't planned on going to that."

"I know you hadn't, you've been dodging my hints all morning. So now I'm asking."

Aurora rolled her eyes, as she got in the car. "I guess so Auntie."

Mrs. Cole smiled and clasped her hands together, "Now that's the spirit. Now one more stop and I'm done with my errands."

As Aurora shifted into drive, she thought to herself, "I was trying to figure out a way around this will, *now* I'm going to have to figure out a way to get away from Auntie Bren."

"Park just over there baby, and come on."

"Oh no ma'am. I'll wait for you in the car."

"Girl, if you don't come on here. I'll only be a minute or two."

"A minute for you is three hours." Aurora said under her breath.

"I heard that Rora Jean." Mrs. Cole snapped."

Aurora burst out laughing. "I'm just saying. Why are we at the church anyway?" She asked as they walked inside.

"Oh, I just need to check on something," she said looking around, "and there he is. I'll be right back."

Aurora's eyes followed Mrs. Cole as she walked toward a man standing next to a table of Christmas decorations. She surveyed him from top to bottom. He was what we would call, 'tall, dark, and handsome.' A very masculine looking man, but there was also a gentleness to him. He looked like he could be a bit older than herself. His walk exuded confidence and leadership, with the kind of eyes you could get lost in. "Mm mm mm, that man is fine."

As she continued to admire the confidence radiating from him and the smoothness in his walk, she realized he was getting closer, walking alongside Mrs. Cole, who had a sly grin on her face.

It was too late for her to turn and walk out of the door, so she just stood there, trying not to look annoyed.

"Baby, won't you come over here and meet our Mayor, Malcolm Mouton."

Aurora cut her eyes at Mrs. Cole and extended her hand to Malcolm. “It’s nice to meet you mayor, I’m Aurora...Aurora Denver.”

"That’s a firm handshake you’ve got there. You must be a business owner. It’s nice to meet you Aurora.”

Aurora smirked, “Really, you got that from my handshake, or did my aunt already tell you all of my business?”

Malcolm raised his hands in surrender. You got me. *But* that really *is* a firm handshake you have.”

“Aurora's going to be with us at the Jubilee,” Mrs. Cole cut in.

“Is she now?” He smiled at Aurora.

Aurora, feeling all of the blood in her body rushing to her cheeks, moved a piece of her hair behind her ear. “Not by choice, Auntie Bren here is basically forcing me to go.”

Malcolm let out a deep laugh. “I definitely know about being forced to do something by Mrs. Cole.”

Aurora lifted her brow, “she forces *you* to do things too? You’re the mayor.”

"It wouldn’t matter if I was the president.” He laughed.

Aurora took notice of how straight and white Malcolm's teeth were and that he had a dimple on his cheek that only showed when he laughed. "Snap out of it Aurora," she thought to herself.

Oh hush." Mrs. Cole interrupted her thoughts." "Things always work out better when you take the wise counsel of your elders."

"You are right about that." Malcolm conceded.

"I know, come on Aurora, I did what I came to do," she said with a smile.

Malcolm shook Aurora's hand again. "It was a pleasure meeting you Aurora. I look forward to seeing you at the jubilee."

"Likewise." Aurora smiled.

"See you later Mayor M&M," Mrs. Cole chuckled.

Malcolm palmed his forehead and ran his hand down his face. "Mrs. Cole," he sighed not hiding his annoyance.

"Mayor M&M? Why'd you call him that?"

"Because he has a hard outer layer, but is just a sweet softy on the inside."

Aurora looked back at Malcolm and smiled. "Hmm"

Chapter Seven

"The Walkins really are a special breed." Aurora laughed as she scrolled through their design pictures Maci emailed over.

"Right," Maci laughed on the other end of the phone. "But they are our top billed clients and keep us entertained throughout the year."

"This is true. I don't even want to know their thoughts with this Jungle Christmas theme they have going. You guys pulled it off masterfully. You all are the dream team of AD Designs."

"Thanks Boss. So how are things progressing there?

Aurora closed her laptop. " No changes, I still have no way around that will, at least not a route I'm willing to take. The town, however, isn't as bad or as small as I thought though. Actually there's a lot here, but it still gives small town vibes. And the people… are pretty decent, I met their mayor… he's ummm nice." she smiled.

"What was that?" Maci interrupted.

"What was what?"

"Did I hear a smile in your voice? Is the mayor hot? Is there a connection? Oooh is he the one you're going to marry?"

"First of all calm down, and no ma'am. I met him once and we talked all of five minutes. My Aunt knows him."

Oh he is FINE!"

"Maci, what are— Did you look him up?"

"Sure did, he's on the website. Girl, forget what I said about your Aunt might mean something else. Marry him."

Aurora laughed. "Maci, that man could be a serial killer."

"He's the mayor, Aurora."

"And? Mayors can commit crimes too."

"Not this one, he's a Godly man."

"Godly men can be serial killers too"

"Correction, those are ungodly men pretending to be Godly, so stop it. Aww he's a widow, with no kids."

"All that is on the town website?"

"Girl, I'm on his Facebook page"

"Oh my God, Maci!"

"I'm just saying boss, if you have to get married to keep that house, might as well be with a man like him."

"And on that note, I am getting off of the phone. By Maci."

Aurora could still hear Maci cracking up as she hung up the phone. Curiosity did get the best of her as she searched his name on Facebook and scrolled through his page.

"Seems like a nice guy though. And that smile!"

She scrolled through a few more pictures. "Let me quit, and get ready for this dang jubilee, Christmas party whatever it is. Besides, I wouldn't dare force this situation on a widower. That'd be cruel."

"Now, that's what I'm talking about." Aurora said with pride as she checked herself out in the mirror.

She was wearing her signature color, a deep plum V-neck jumper with a silver belt, diamond teardrop earrings with a matching necklace. Her curls were pulled up into a high messy bun, with a few loose strands hanging, and light make up with a silver clutch.

She sprayed on her Valentino perfume and grabbed her keys as the doorbell rang.

"Whoa. Don't you look fabulous Auntie Bren," she said when she opened the door.

"You act like you're surprised. Your taste and fashion didn't just come from Celeste, you know." She teased throwing her scarf over her shoulder.

"Yes ma'am. You know I was going to pick you up at your house."

"I know. I wanted to make sure you grab the right coat. And I was hoping you'd wear this outfit tonight.'

Aurora narrowed her eyes. "Auntie, what are you up to?"

"Nothing child, now let's go."

As she drove to the banquet hall downtown near the dock, Aurora couldn't help but wonder if Mrs. Cole was trying to play matchmaker. "Does she know what auntie mom left in her will? As nosy as she is, she never really asked me about it."

Thoughts were going through her head she hadn't heard her aunt call her name.

"Rora Jean, snap out of it child."

"My apologies auntie. I have a lot on my mind."

Mrs. Cole tilted her head. "I see. We're going to talk about that soon, but right now, let's go have a good time."

Aurora feigned a smile. " yes ma'am."

They walked into a beautifully decorated banquet hall. It was overflowing with Christmas decorations and high spirited people. Everyone was laughing and having a good time. Children were running in between chairs, there were servers walking around with trays of drinks. All different size tables were set up, some round, some square, but still surprisingly coordinated.

Some people were up dancing, and some were standing out on the patio. It was lightly snowing, and yet they seemed unfazed by it.

Mrs. Cole ushered her to a cluster of round tables, and they took their seats. In came the flood of 'nice to meet yous' and good to see you agains'.

Feeling overstimulated by all of the questions and small talk, Aurora excuse herself and walk toward the patio, grabbing a glass of wine on the way.

Taking a sip, "of course it's non-alcoholic," she laughs as she makes her way outside.

She continues to walk, feigning a smile at the party-goers she passes, until she ends up, walking away from the party and to the docks.

Looking out at the waves crashing against the docks, she takes a deep breath and lets out a large sigh. She watches as the snowflakes disappear on the water and stick to the railings.

"What's the matter, too small for a big city girl like you?" A smoothe voice says from behind her.

She turns to face Malcolm, who's wearing a deep burgundy suit that complemented her dress.

"No," she smiled. "I just needed some fresh air and quiet from that rambunctious group in there. The real question is, are you stalking me, Mr. Mayor?"

Malcolm chuckled. “Of course not. Mrs. Cole sent me to come check on you.”

"Of course she did. Nice suit by the way.”

He smoothed his hands down his blazer. “You think so? It wasn’t my first choice, but someone *insisted* I wear it.”

"I can only imagine who that someone is.” She looked toward the banquet hall.

Malcolm just smiled. “You, however, look great. Purple really suits you.”

"Thank you.” She smile, turning her gaze back to the water.

"So, what do you think of our town?”

Aurora smile faded, and stayed locked on the waves crashing. “Under different circumstances, I’d actually love it here. I’m used to the fast pace of Boston, but this place is kind of starting to grow on me. Plus, it is where I was raised.”

Malcolm leaned over the railing. “What circumstances, if you don’t mind me asking?”

"Well," Aurora shifted. " it's just weird being here without my Aunt Celeste. I really miss her, more so, the time I could have spent here with her."

"You're Miss Celeste's niece?"

Aurora looked up at him. " Yes, you knew her?"

"Everyone did. Miss Celeste was a really great woman. I'm sorry. I can only imagine how you feel. I lost my wife a few years ago. It can be tough, but the ache gets easier to bear. Trust me."

"Thank you for that. I really appreciate it."

"Of course."

A silence fell between them.

"Aurora, I don't want to seem too forward, but would you like to have dinner with me?"

Aurora raised an eyebrow. "Did My aunt put you up to this? She already has us color coordinated. I can't believe her."

"No, she didn't promise." Malcolm chuckled. "Although, I do give her an A for effort."

"Oh" Aurora relaxed. "Well....yes, I'd like that."

"Great. Now, how about we head back in, before we both freeze."

"Actually, could you make sure my aunt gets home. I'm going to take off."

"I can do that, everything okay?"

"Yes, I'm just partied out."

"Okay, well, I'll walk you to your car."

"Thank you Malcolm, I'm okay though. I'm sure they are missing the mayor in there."

"They'll be fine. Are you sure you don't want me to walk you? I don't mind."

"I'm sure. Good night, Malcolm."

"Good night, Aurora." Malcolm watched until she was in her car and pulling out of the parking lot before he returned to the party.

Aurora finished brushing her teeth, grabbed her phone to text Maci, then changed her mind and tossed it on the bed.

"Aaargh." She snatched a stuffed bear, sat in the bay window, snuggling with it, and and stared out at the lake.

"I didn't realize just how much I missed this view."

Her phone buzzed on the bed, and for once she didn't rush to grab it. She just let it ring.

Her thoughts drifted back to Malcolm. " He's such a nice guy. Ah ah. You've only talked to him twice now. Besides your focus is this house."

Her phone buzzed again.

This time she got up, put it on the charger, got in the bed and went to sleep.

Chapter Eight

Taking a sip of her coffee, Aurora scrolled through commercial property listings. She occasionally looked up, observing other customers. Tiana's bistro has become her regular morning spot.

"Sooo, how'd your dinner date go?" Maci giggled on the phone.

Aurora sighed. "It wasn't a date Maci, we just had dinner."

"Did he pick you up?"

"No, I met him there."

"Typical." Maci snorted..

"Watch it." Aurora laughed.

"Fine, it wasn't a date, how was dinner?"

"It was nice. I just don't want to get anything started while I'm trying to figure this whole situation out."

"That does make sense. So when do you think you'll be back? Or are you going to stay there through February?"

Aurora was silent for a bit as she stared at her laptop screen. "I was actually thinking about setting up a second office here."

Maci gasped. "Have my ears deceived me, or are you beginning to plant roots?"

"Well, if I'm going to be here for the next few months, I'm going to need an office to work out of. You know I don't do work from home well."

"Don't I know it." Maci laughed.

"Hush. But to be quite honest. I'm actually beginning to feel at home here. I've been sleeping better and not as glued to my laptop and phone."

"Would you look at that. I told you it could do you some good. Do you want me to scout some places for an office space for you?"

"No. I found something in the Heights area, it's their business district and it's a pretty great area."

"Sounds like you have already made up your mind."

"Not completely, just planning ahead. I think— oh shoot. My aunt just walked in, I'll talk to you later."

Maci laughed. "Are you *still* avoiding her? *Aurora*."

"Yeah if you ever meet her, you'll see why." She laughed "got to go."

Aurora started packing up her laptop to try and further avoid Mrs. Cole. She hadn't talk to her since she left her at the town Christmas party. She was still irritated with her for trying to set her up with Malcolm.

"Hello young lady." Mrs. Cole greeted her as she was getting ready to walk out. " You know, it's not every day I get stranded at a Christmas party."

Aurora rolled her eyes. "Auntie Bren, I love you, but I am not in the mood. Besides you weren't stranded, *the mayor* brought you home." She said walking passed her and out of the door.

Mrs. Cole followed her out. "Now you wait a minute. You were raised better than that. What is wrong with you child?"

Aurora spun round on the sidewalk. "Nothing is wrong, Auntie, and I apologize for snapping, but sometimes, respectfully, I wish you would just mind your business. You had that man dress in a color to match *me* and *then* sent him to ask me out! Why would you do that?"

"I meant no harm baby, I just thought you two would hit it off, he's a respectful and God-fearing man. And I didn't tell him to ask you out. I didn't know he had."

"And what makes you think I want that? That I would even want to be here? My home is in Boston, not here Aunt Bren. I'm only here because..."

"Because what baby?"

"Never mind. Auntie, please just stop pushing. I will see you later. I don't have the mental bandwidth for this." Wiping a tear, she gets in her car and drives off.

Aurora sat in her Aunt Celeste's favorite chair near the fire place, locked in a memory of when she would sit here, but on the floor every morning before school while Celeste platted her hair. She ran her hands through her, hair remembering how she would playfully tease her about cutting it off.

She wrapped herself more in the blanket she pulled out of Celeste's closet, took in a deep breath and sighed.

"Okay God. I'm trying this again. What is the lesson I'm supposed to be learning in all this, and why did I have to come all the way here to learn it? You know I am no good at this prayer thing. Auntie Mom would would tell me prayer is just a conversation with you....Come on God. It's Christmas, can I get some kind of answers?" She pleads.

The house is silent and Aurora stares into the fireplace, watching the flames flicker. She'd begun to drift to sleep when she heard a soft knock on the door. She stood up and stretched, then opened the door.

"Merry Christmas baby." Mrs. Cole walked in with bags in her hand. "Help with me with these would you." She hands a few of them to Aurora and heads to the kitchen.

"Auntie what's all this?" She follows behind her.

She starts pulling food and decorations out of the bags. "You didn't think I was going to let you spend Christmas alone did you?

"I kind of did. I was a bit rude to you the other day. I'm sorry about that by the way."

Mrs. Cole smiled. "Yes you were rude, but I wouldn't be who I was if I let you stay in here by yourself on Christmas. Now come help me trim this bare tree of yours."

Aurora laughed, "Yes ma'am," and turned on a Christmas playlist while they decorated the tree in the living room.

The day went on as they laughed, danced, shared stories and ate the food Mrs. Cole brought over.

After they finished dinner Mrs. Cole grabbed a gift bag from the tree. "I have something for you baby." And handed the bag to her.

"Auntie you didn't have to get me anything, plus I didn't buy a gift for you."

"Never you mind that, just open it."

She opened her gift and gasped. "Auntie, this is beautiful. Oh my gosh," she started at the stunning emerald jewelry set-complete with matching earrings, necklace, and bracelet.

"I figured I'd add to your collection of jewelry." She smiled. "Oh I love it!"

"I'm glad baby. Now open this one."

"Another one?" She giggled like a kid.

When she opened the box, her eyes widened with shock. She looked up at Mrs. Cole with tears in her eyes, then looked back at the antique music box.

"Do you recognize it?"

Aurora shook her head unable to speak.

"Celeste had it repaired before she died. She told me to hold on to it and let God tell me when to give it to you. I was on my way over here when He told me to go back in and get it. So there you are."

Aurora smiled as she turned the crank on the box and it began to play it's melody. I haven't heard this in *so* long, not since I broke it the week before I left for Boston. She didn't talk to me that entire week."

"I've never known Celeste to be mad, let alone hold a grudge."

Aurora looked up. "She was more disappointed then mad. It was the only thing she had of my mom and I acted like I didn't care when I dropped it."

Mrs. Cole grabbed Aurora's hand gently. "It wasn't about the music box baby. She was sad that you were leaving. She knew once you got to Boston, she was going to see you less and less."

Aurora put her head down, "I just wanted to make something of myself, like she did. I just wanted to make her proud."

"You did, she was very proud of you. She bragged to anyone whom would listen about her big city niece and all you accomplished."

Aurora stood up abruptly. "If she was *so* proud Auntie, then why did she force me to come back here. Not only that, beyond the grave she is forcing me to get married. Why would she do that?

"She what? What are you taking about?"

"Like you don't know. Isn't that why you tried to set me up with the mayor?"

Aurora calm down. I have no idea what you are talking about."

"Oh no?" She stormed off into her bedroom looking through her paperwork. She came back in, handing her the copy of Celeste's will. "There. It's all right there. In order for me to inherit this house, I have to be married by Valentine's Day. I had to come here, stay through the holiday and get married. I could let the house go on market and try to buy it back, but that's iffy too. So marriage it is. This is basically a shot gun wedding. No pressure right?"

"Aurora."

"That's why I didn't want to get involved with Malcolm. He's a nice guy and I'm not trying to trap anyone."

"Aurora."

"Ugh, this just so unfair."

"AURORA."

"Ma'am?"

"Did you read this?"

"Of course I did, many times. I even had a local lawyer look at it. She said it's no way around it."

"Well that part is true, but did you ask her about the marriage?"

"I didn't have to auntie, it's right there. Why are you acting like I don't know how to read a legal document?"

Mrs. Cole looked up at Aurora. "Come have a seat," she patted the couch cushion next to her.

Aurora obliged and sat down.

“Now I want you to take three deep breaths, exhale slowly and clear your mind.”

“Auntie why—"

"Just do it, Rora Jean.”

Aurora sat back, closed her eyes, and followed Mrs. Cole’s instructions. With each breath, her shoulders relaxed and her body loosened up, then she opened her eyes.

“Now read this to me, out loud.” She handed her the will.

My beloved Aurora,

I have asked that you return to Eden's Harbour and remain through the winter season, no later than Valentine's Day.

By then, i trust you will have made a binding decision about the life you intend to live going forward.

This home may only pass to you once you are no longer living solely for yourself, but are prepared to share your life in a way that is visible, witnessed, and permanent.

I will not leave this house to you while your life remains unanchored, with every door left open and every attachment is optional.

By the close of this season, i expect you to know whether you are willing to stand beside someone or continue to stand alone.

Should you find yourself unable or unwilling to make such a commitment by then, you are free to return to the life you have built elsewhere without judgment, regret, or wondering what if.

With all my love

Auntie Mom

Aurora puts down the letter, "So she mean it. Valentine's Day was clear."

Mrs. Cole softens a bit more. "Baby...where did she say anything bout a husband?

Aurora blinks, processing what she just read. She realizes she never said husband, married, or wedding. She had filled that in herself.

She looks back down at the will and slowly re-reads a line and holds her breath.

"Baby...Celeste would never force you to get married." Mrs. Cole says softly.

Aurora exhales and cries.

Mrs. Cole pulls her into an embrace, rubbing the back of her head. "It's okay baby."

"I've been so mad at her," she continues to cry, "I thought she was giving me an ultimatum."

"Oh baby no," she wipes the tears from Auroras cheeks, "your aunt in all of her wisdom, was giving you an invitation."

"But why all the legalities and how did I even misread what was written. "Would you have come back on your own?"

Aurora looks down.

"That's why." She laughed. "And the mind can be a tricky thing. You were grieving and I'm sure only focused in on certain phrases. From there your mind created a narrative and that's all you could see or hear."

"I can see that happening, but why the winter season?"

“I’m sure she chose this time because the town has so many events from November to February, you’d get a chance to experience it at it’s peak, and meet a good bit of people. Not to mention she kept tabs on you and knew this season is your slowest at work.”

Aurora looked up surprised. “How’d she know that?”

"She had her ways,” she smiled.

"Maci,” she palmed her forehead. “Is that why she said, it may not mean what I think it means, when I told her about the will?”

Mrs. Cole chuckled. “Smart girl, that Maci, and such a sweetheart.”

"So everyone knew but me?”

"You had your path to walk baby. You had to get here on your own or else you wouldn't have accepted it. What you do with this revelation is up to you. “Now,” she rose up from her seat. “I’m going to go home and get some rest.”

"Okay Auntie Bren, thank you again for my gifts and helping me to see clearly.”

"Don’t thank me baby, thank the good Lord, this is all his doing. I’ll see you later.” She kissed her cheek and walked out the door.

Aurora sits in the silence realizing just how much she had been stressing herself. All because she allowed her emotions to lead her.

Chapter Nine

The crisp morning air blew across Aurora's face as she watched the sunrise from the pier.

"As long as I've lived here, I still never get tired of seeing the sunrise over the ocean." A familiar voice came up behind her.

"It really is beautiful. Good morning Mayor." She smiled.

Malcolm handed her a coffee. "Good morning Aurora."

"She took a sip and it was perfect. "I see you're stalking me again."

"Maybe you're the one stalking me." He smiled. "I'm always here to see God light the day."

"Mhmm."she looks passed him. "I see you all are already gearing up for the new year."

"Yes ma'am, the festivities continue here throughout the year here in the harbor. You plan on sticking around?"

"I haven't fully decided yet, but I am leaning toward a maybe."

"Maybe, huh?"

"Yep, maybe." She takes a long sip of her coffee.

"I guess I'll have to take that as a challenge to turn that maybe into a yes."

Aurora walked further down the pier away from him, but turned and smiled. "I guess you will, *Mayor.*" She turned, continuing her walk to the further end of he pier.

"Alright then," Malcolm smiled as he walked toward City Hall. "Challenge accepted."

"You know God, you could have just said I needed to slow down. You didn't have to have my family and friends conspire to get me down here." She laughed watching the waves crash.

"As glamorous of a life Auntie Mom had, I'm starting to see why she settled down here. I'm still not sure if I will, but I am definitely starting to see the appeal."

As the snow began to fall again, Aurora pulled the hood of her coat over her head and walked back to her car.

“I guess I *could* stay another month or two.” She pulled out her phone and dialed Maci.

“Hey Maci. How do you feel about coming to Maine for a month? She smiled as Maci shrieked on the other end.

“I’m already packed and booking a flight!”

Aurora drove home with a better outlook on what was ahead. She may not have made the decision to stay in Eden’s Harbour, but she was more open to it now that she knows she’s not being forced to be here.

Who knows what the New Year may bring........

A New Kind of
New Year

A KINDRED HEARTS STORY

T. LAWREN

The town always looked different at the end of December.

The holidays in Eden's Harbour always seemed like the setting of a movie, picture perfect. Evergreen wreaths still clinging to front doors, twinkle lights refusing to come down too soon, and snow dusting the sidewalks as if the Lord Himself had taken His time smoothing everything over.

Imani Mouton stood at the wide front windows of her studio, arms folded loosely over her chest, watching the last students trickle out into the cold.

“See you next week, Miss Imani!” a little girl called, her voice muffled by the thick scarf wrapped around her face.

Imani smiled. “You better. And don’t forget, stretch, stretch, stretch.”

The girl giggled and skipped off toward her mother.

When the door clicked shut behind them, the studio finally fell silent.

It was an eerie silence that she would always try to fill with noise, just so she wouldn't have to sit inside her own thoughts.

Now, she began to welcome the silence as a challenge to get through her days.

The empty studio held echoes of who she used to be.

She turned slowly, taking in the space.

The pale wood floors she'd fought for.

The mirrors she'd paid for herself.

The soft white curtains she'd hung one summer afternoon when her life still felt...full.

The ballet studio had been hers long before she ever became someone's wife.

Long before she became someone's ex-wife.

It had always been *hers*.

And somehow, that mattered more now than it ever had before.

Imani reached for her phone, scrolling absently until she saw the notification she'd ignored all day

Big Brother: You coming tonight? Don't make me come get you.

Imani scoffed softly, shaking her head.

Although her brother was the mayor of Eden's Harbour, to her, he was just big brother.

She typed back quickly:

Yessss. I will be there. Quit asking.

A pause.

Then:

Oh and Mrs. Cole wants you to sit with her. Be ready for an interrogation.

Imani laughed—an actual laugh, surprised by how easily it came.

Mrs. Cole had that effect on people, she was the sweetest, nosiest, God loving lady in the town, and she adored her.

She had a way of looking at you like she already knew what God was doing in your life...even when you were still pretending you didn't.

Imani set her phone down and walked toward the small office tucked in the back corner of the studio. Her coat hung neatly on the hook, alongside a tiny scarf one of her daughters had knitted in school.

Her daughters.

Her heart softened immediately.

Everything she did circled back to them.

For so long, she'd convinced herself that being strong meant being everything for everyone else.

A good wife.

A good mother.

A good teacher.

A good daughter.

A good sister.

A good woman.

But somewhere in the unraveling of her marriage...in the quiet aftermath of signing papers and dividing years of their lives, Imani had realized something that shook her more than the divorce ever did.

She had been trying so hard to keep the peace...

That she had forgotten herself.

Not lost her faith.

Not lost her joy.

Just...

Forgotten that she was allowed to be whole, too.

Imani slipped her coat on slowly, fingers brushing the gold bracelet around her wrist.

A small reminder of what she still had.

A life and a future.

A new year sitting right in front of her and she was ready to take it on with a different outlook.

She turned off the studio lights, locking the door behind her.

The town's glow stretched ahead, quiet and inviting.

Somewhere nearby, Eden's Harbour was gathering as it always did—warm drinks, prayer, laughter, a countdown to another new year.

And for the first time in a long time...

Imani wasn't stepping into this new year trying to prove anything.

She was stepping into it with one simple decision settled deep in her chest.

This year...she would put herself first.

Because her girls deserved the best version of their mother.

And she deserved the very best of herself.

Imani pulled her scarf tighter and started walking.

The snow crunched beneath her boots.

She looked toward the sky and smiled. This New Year, she was taking back control of her life.

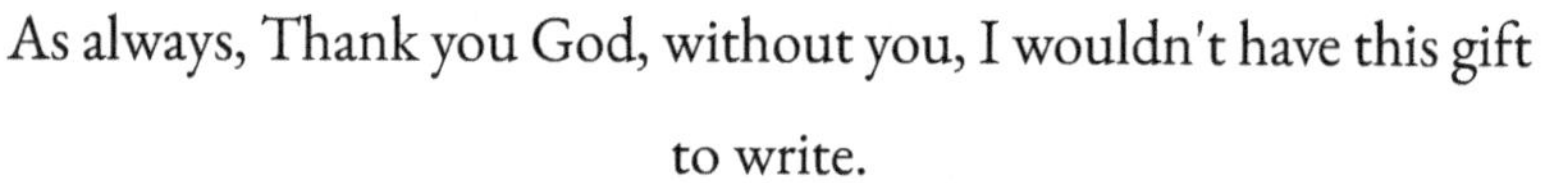

As always, Thank you God, without you, I wouldn't have this gift to write.

A special thank you to my leaders for your continuous encouragement, prayers and love.

And to my Daddy. You are forever missed, thank you for showing me so much love that I am able to write that into my characters. Your love lives on through me and through the father figures I create in books.

T. Lawren is a Southeast Texas native and faith-based author and speaker dedicated to helping others rediscover their identity, reconnect with God, and boldly walk in purpose.

A lifelong lover of reading and writing, she felt the call to publish her first book in her late 30s, reminding others that it's never too late to start something new.

Through her transformative works like *The Path to Purpose* and its Reflection Guide, she encourages readers to embrace healing, spiritual growth, and intentional living, one page at a time. Alongside her nonfiction work, she also writes Christian fiction, weaving stories that offer hope, connection, and faith-filled insight.

Her writing speaks to individuals navigating life's transitions, reminding them that their story still matters.

www.ingramcontent.com/pod-product-compliance
Lightning Source LLC
LaVergne TN
LVHW010356160826
845677LV00005BA/1296

9798992807769